A LITTLE SAFETY SPOT

SCHOOL

STOP

AT SCHOOL

To my children, Ryan and Anna

This SAFETY book belongs to:

_____

_____

_____

STOP! SAFETY SPOTS ARE HERE! Have you had your SCHOOL SAFETY training yet?

It is important that we are SAFE when we learn, play, and have fun! So, the other SAFETY SPOTS and I are here to show you how you can be SAFE AT SCHOOL!

LOOK! The SAFETY SPOTS are already SPOTTING SAFE SITUATIONS!

When crossing the street, it's important to always LOOK for cars and cyclists. You can do this by, looking left, looking right, and then looking left again!!

Adults can see things that you may not, that's why it's important to HOLD HANDS before entering the street!

LOOK LEFT.

LOOK RIGHT.

LOOK LEFT, AGAIN.

There are a lot of ways to be SAFE INSIDE of a school bus.

Keep your hands and feet INSIDE the bus.

Use inside voices.

No eating food.

Okay, now that we've talked about safety outside of the school, it's time to go INSIDE the SCHOOL to see all the ways you can **be SAFE!**

When you are INSIDE the school, ALWAYS use walking feet.

Use the handrail when walking up or down stairs.

Be on the look out for safety signs, to prevent injury.

If an accident happens, tell a teacher right away.

Stay with your class, so you don't get lost.

Some THINGS need to be handled safely.
Scissor SAFETY needs to be used ALL THE TIME!

Make sure your shoes
are tied, so you don't trip.

Lunchtime is full of SAFETY SPOTS!
Throwing away your trash is
a great way to be RESPECTFUL, RESPONSIBLE,
and SAFE!

Remember to
ONLY EAT YOUR OWN FOOD
and eat QUIETLY and SLOWLY, so you
don't choke.

If you see this sign
make sure to keep
peanuts away.
This protects people
with food allergies.

Peanut-Free Zone

Please do not
bring any peanuts
or products
containing peanuts
into this area.

When drinking
water from the
fountain, don't
put your mouth
on the spout.

There are a lot of germs at school and we all
want to stay healthy. So, it's important to
COVER YOUR MOUTH WHEN YOU COUGH!
Cough or sneeze into your sleeve or
a tissue to avoid spreading germs.

Don't forget to
throw away your
tissue after.

It's important to wash your hands, after using the bathroom and before you eat, to avoid getting sick.

Make sure you use soap.

Wash your hands for at least 20 seconds (sing happy birthday twice).

If you are feeling pressured to do something you don't want to do or you think is wrong, have the courage to say NO.

If you see someone being treated unkindly, ask them if they need help. If they do, get the teacher.

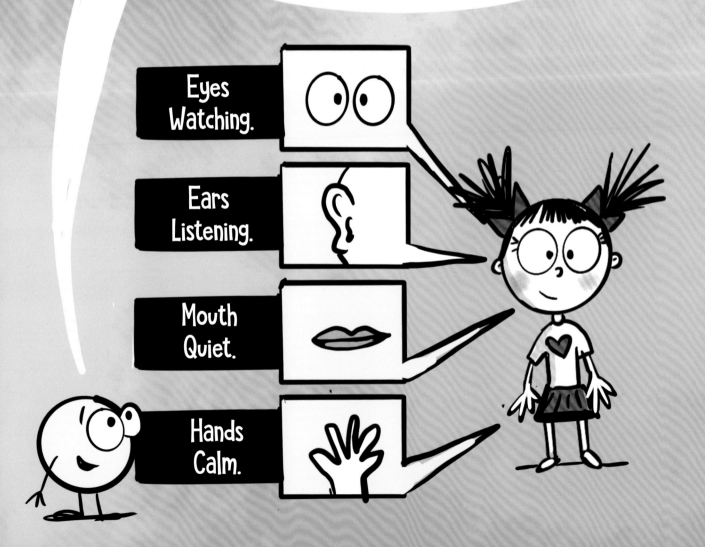

FIRE

STOP

Stop what you are doing.

Get in Line.

Walk to our safe spot. You might see a firefighter. They are there to keep us safe.

INTRUDER

STOP

Stop what you are doing.

Walk to our safe spot.

The teacher will shut off the lights. Sit together quietly. You might see the police. They are there to keep us safe.

EARTH QUAKE

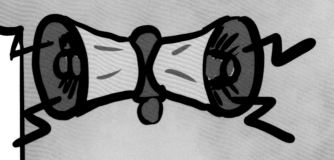

STOP what you are doing.

Crawl under a table or desk.

Crouch down and hold the table legs.

During the DRILLS, stay CALM and listen to your teacher.

If you feel scared or worried during the DRILL, remember your teacher is there to keep you safe.

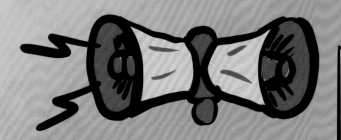

After the drill is over, wait for your teacher's instruction to go back to what you were doing.

Be proud of yourself for staying SAFE and practicing drills

TORNADO

 Stop what you are doing.

Get in Line.

Walk to our safe spot.

Crouch into a ball and cover your head.

We hope you enjoyed SPOTTING SAFETY with us today! SAFETY is everyone's responsibility and if we all make an effort to be safe, then it will make the world a better place.

PERSONAL SAFETY INFORMATION

My full name is: _____

My age is: _____

My siblings names are: _____

My address is:
_____
_____

My emergency contact person's number is:

☐☐☐ - ☐☐☐ - ☐☐☐☐

I made this card especially for you. In an emergency, community helpers might need this information from you so it's good to have it memorized.

This "Personal Safety Information" card is FREE for download on www.dianealber.com, so children can practice knowing their information.